Also by Kathryn O. Galbraith

KATIE DID!
illustrated by Ted Ramsey

SOMETHING SUSPICIOUS

WAITING FOR JENNIFER
illustrated by Irene Trivas

(Margaret K. McElderry Books)

ROOMMATES

Kathryn O. Galbraith
illustrated by Mark Graham

Enjoy!

Kathryn O. Galbraith

Margaret K. McElderry Books
NEW YORK

Margaret K. McElderry Books
Macmillan Publishing Company
866 Third Avenue
New York, New York 10022
Collier Macmillan Canada, Inc.

Printed in the United States of America
10 9 8 7 6 5 4 3 2

Library of Congress Cataloging-in-Publication Data
Galbraith, Kathryn Osebold.
Roommates / Kathryn O. Galbraith; illustrated by Mark Graham. — 1st ed.
p. cm.
Summary: When Mama announces a new baby is on the way who will need a separate room, two sisters become roommates.
ISBN 0-689-50487-X
[1. Sisters—Fiction. 2. Roommates—Fiction.]
I. Graham, Mark, 1952- ill. II. Title.
PZ7.G1303Ro 1990 [E]—dc20 89-33434 CIP AC

To the Roommates and their cousin—
Elissa, Amy, Jenny, and Jessica.
And once again to my roommate, Steve.
K.O.G.

Chapter One

It was Saturday. Mimi was in her room, reading a book.

Beth was in her room. She was playing with Willie.

"Girls," Mama called. "I'm going to paint the baby's crib. Do you want to help?"

"Sure," said Mimi.

"Sure," said Beth.

Mimi spread the newspaper on the floor. Beth helped stir the yellow paint.

Mama smiled. "Just think," she said. "Soon the baby will be here."

Mimi looked at the crib. It was very big.

Beth looked at it too. "Where's the baby going to sleep?" she asked.

"Not in my room," said Mimi. She didn't want a big baby's bed in her room.

"Not in my room either," Beth said quickly.

They both looked at Mama.

"New babies cry a lot," Mama began.

Mimi and Beth nodded.

"And new babies need their diapers changed."

"Diapers!" Mimi held her nose. "Not in my room."

"Soooo," Mama said. "You two girls will have to move in together."

Mimi looked at Beth. Beth looked at Mimi.

"TOGETHER!"

"But Mimi's so messy!"

"Beth pinches!"

Mama didn't seem to hear.

"Yes, together. You'll be roommates."

"Whose room are we going to move into?" asked Beth.

"Mine!" said Mimi. "I'm the oldest. Besides, my room is bigger."

"That's not fair," Beth said. "You're always the oldest."

Mama shook her head. "No, Mimi is right. Her room is a little bigger. I think you should move into Mimi's room."

"Ha!" Mimi whispered to Beth. "I told you so."

After lunch, Daddy moved Beth's bed into Mimi's room.

Mimi looked around. Now her

room looked very small.

Beth carried in all her toys. Mimi's room looked even smaller.

Beth looked around. "Mimi, you are so messy. You have to clean up your stuff."

"No I don't," Mimi said. "This is my room."

Daddy said, "Mimi, Beth is right. This room belongs to both of you now."

"Ha!" whispered Beth. "I told you so."

On Tuesday Beth asked Heather to come over and play. Mimi sat on her bed and teased them.

"Do you want to play dolls or dress-up?" Beth asked Heather.

"Do you want to play dolls or dress-up?" Mimi repeated.

"Stop it, Mimi," Beth said.

"Stop it, Mimi," Mimi said.

"Mama," Beth called. "Mimi is teasing us. Make her stop."

"Mimi," Mama called. Her voice was tired. "Stop teasing your sister."

"I'm not teasing her," Mimi said. "I'm just talking out loud!"

Mimi had Brownies on Thursday. After Brownies, Kelly came home with her. Mimi and Kelly sat on Mimi's bed. They ate peanut-butter-and-jelly crackers.

Beth sat on her bed. She ate peanut-butter-and-jelly crackers too.

"Go away, copycat!" Mimi said. "Kelly and I want to talk."

"I don't have to," Beth said. "This is my room too."

"Mama, Beth is bothering us," Mimi called.

"No I'm not," Beth called back. "I'm not saying a word."

Beth pretended to read her

book. She was so quiet the girls forgot to whisper.

"I think Timothy is cute," Kelly said.

Mimi giggled. "I think Danny is cuter!"

That night in bed Beth sang, "Mimi has a boyfriend! Mimi has a boyfriend!"

"I do not!" Mimi shouted.

"Girls, go to sleep," Mama called. "I don't want to hear another word from you tonight."

That was okay with Mimi. She rolled over and closed her eyes tight. She didn't want to hear another word from Beth... ever!

Chapter Three

Beth went into the kitchen. She held up her spelling book. "Mama, can you help me?"

"I'll help you after dinner," Mama said. "I'm busy now."

Daddy was in the garden. He was weeding the roses.

"Daddy, can you help me?"

"Not right now, honey. I'll

help you after dinner, okay?"

Beth marched into her room. "After dinner, after dinner," she said to Mimi. "Everybody says 'after dinner'! I need help right now!"

"I'll help you," Mimi said. She put down Willie's brush.

Beth looked at her. "You will?"

"Sure," Mimi said. "I'll be the teacher. You and Willie can be in my class."

Mimi said each spelling word very slowly. Very slowly, Beth spelled each word back.

"Here's the last one," Mimi said. "Yellow."

"Y-E-L-L-O-W," spelled Beth.

"Very good," Mimi said. She

sounded just like Mrs. Wheeler, Beth's teacher.

Beth gave a skip. "Thanks, Mimi."

The next day Mimi ran all the way home from school. "I'm in the Thanksgiving play!" she shouted.

"Are you an Indian?" asked Beth.

Mimi smiled. She shook her head.

"Are you a Pilgrim?" Mama asked.

Mimi shook her head again. She held up her costume. It was yellow in the front. It was green on the sides. At the top were strands of yellow yarn.

"I know!" Beth said. "You're an ear of corn."

Mimi nodded. "I am a gift from the Indians," she said. She showed

Beth and Mama her speech. "I tell the Pilgrims all about the new land."

That night, just before bedtime, Mimi said, "Beth, would you help me?"

Beth sat up in bed. "Sure," she said.

Beth listened to Mimi's speech. Beth listened again in the morning. She listened to it

every night. Soon Mimi and
Beth could say the speech together:

"This is a land of many lakes.
This is a land of many trees.
This is a land of valleys and
mountains.
This is a land of freedom."

Wednesday was the school
play. Mimi remembered every
word of her speech. Beth was so
proud.

That night, Mimi and Beth
sang:

"This is a land of many lakes.
This is a land of many trees.
This is a land of valleys and
mountains.
This is a land of freeeeeeedom!"

Chapter Four

"Mama," said Beth. "I don't feel good." Beth's head was hot, her hands were cold.

"I think it's the flu," Mama said. She helped Beth into bed.

On Saturday Beth felt worse than ever. Mimi tiptoed over to her bed. "Here, Beth." Mimi held out her pink shell necklace. "You can wear this."

The next day Mimi got the flu too. Mimi's head hurt. Beth's tummy ached.

"I hate the flu," Beth said. "It's horrible! Terrible!"

"Gross!" Mimi said.

But getting over the flu

together was fun. Mimi and Beth played hospital with Willie.

"Here, Willie. Let us fix your broken leg."

"Here, Willie. Let us fix your broken tail."

At last Willie wiggled away.

"I know," said Mimi. "Let's play pirates!"

Mama brought them glasses of orange juice. She looked at their pirate-ship bed. "What a mess!" she said. Then she smiled. "But I'm glad you are feeling better!"

That night Mimi and Beth played their favorite guessing game.

"Guess what the baby will be," said Mimi. "A boy or a girl?"

Beth hated guessing first. "Uh . . . a boy," she said.

Now it was Mimi's turn. "A girl," Mimi said.

"Wait," Beth said. "I mean, a girl too."

"Copycat!" Mimi said.

"I am not!" Beth said. Beth decided never to talk to Mimi again.

Mimi didn't seem to notice. "If it is a girl," Mimi said, "we can call her Ramona." Then she giggled. "Or if it's a boy, we can call him Danny."

Beth forgot she wasn't talking to Mimi. "I hope it's a girl," she said. She liked "Ramona" better than "Danny."

"Having a little sister would be fun," Mimi agreed.

Beth sat up. "Do you really

think little sisters are fun?"

Mimi nodded. "Uh-huh, sometimes."

Beth hugged her knees. Soon I'll be a big sister, she thought. And I'm going to be a big sister just like Mimi . . . sometimes.

Chapter Five

It was one week after Thanksgiving. Mimi and Beth came out of school. They looked for Mama's car.

"Mimi! Beth!" It was Daddy.

They ran over to the car.

"Where's Mama?" Beth asked.

"Does she have the flu?" Mimi asked.

Daddy shook his head. He was smiling. "No. Guess what? You have a new baby sister!"

"Really?" Mimi shouted. "A baby sister!"

"What does she look like?" asked Beth.

Daddy laughed. "Beautiful! Just like her big sisters!"

To celebrate, Daddy took them out to dinner. "You can order anything you like," he said.

"I'll have chicken," Mimi said.

"Uh, I'll have chicken too," Beth said. She looked at Mimi.

For once Mimi didn't say "copycat." She was too happy.

Then Mimi remembered something. "What's the new

baby's name?" she asked.

"We're going to call her Rachel," Daddy said. "What do you girls think of that?"

"Rachel is a pretty name," Beth said.

Mimi thought a minute. Then she nodded. Rachel was a pretty name. And maybe they could call her Rachel Ramona. She would ask Mama tomorrow. Rachel Ramona would be a *really* pretty name.

That night Daddy went to visit Mama and Rachel. Mrs. Fletcher came to stay with Mimi and Beth.

"Good night, girls," she said. She turned off the light. "Sleep tight."

Mimi and Beth were too excited to sleep.

"A baby sister!" Mimi whispered. "I can't wait to see her."

"Someday," Beth said, "I'm going to teach her how to dance."

"Someday," Mimi said, "I'm going to teach her how to...to be an ear of corn!"

Mimi and Beth laughed.

"Shh, girls," Mrs. Fletcher called. "Go to sleep."

Mimi lay down.

Beth lay down too. Then she sat up. "Look." She bumped Mimi's bed with her foot. "The moon has a smile on its face."

Mimi looked out the window. "It does!"

"You know what?" Beth whispered. "Maybe someday Rachel can sleep in here too."

Mimi nodded. "Then we can all be roommates together."

Roommates. Mimi liked the sound of that word. Lots of kids had to share a room, but having a roommate was special.

"Good night, Mimi. Good night, moon," Beth called.

Mimi giggled. "Good night, roommate."